TRAPPED

a tryst with life

ANSH JAVERI

ISBN
978-1-4828-8522-4
978-1-4828-8523-1

Print information available on the last page.

To order additional copies of this book, contact
Partridge India
000 800 10062 62
www.partridgepublishing.com/india
orders.india@partridgepublishing.com

08/31/2016

PARTRIDGE

CHAPTER I

I stood there, being yelled by my superior. He yelled and yelled but then suddenly everything seemed to stop. That's what I thought had happened but when I saw closely, I realized everything was moving in slow motion. I walked towards him; surprisingly I was normal. I could see all of his spittle coming out of his mouth as I said, "Gross". Feeling disgusted.

Suddenly, an extremely bright light shone from above blinding everything. And then, the ground beneath me gave away forming a circle.

I fell down a deep pit filled with beasts. Dropping multiple levels, I could see them holding a creepy looking trident, screaming and shouting at me all the time, "YOUR'E A LOSER, A FAILURE, YOU COULDN'T DO YOUR JOB".

I suddenly woke up with no idea where I was and with the words coming from my mouth, "NO"!! I realize that I'm in my apartment, my sweet little apartment. Thank god it was a Nightmare. It happens to me every night, making me an insomniac. I sit up, put the bed sheet aside and stand up. I walk towards the door and look at my reflection in the mirror hanging on the front door. I could see that I was a complete mess. I look at the reflection of the clock behind me and the time shows 7:50 a.m. "I'm a dead guy, today's the worst day of my life". I rushed to the bathroom and start to dress up.

My name is Adam Robertson. I'm working in the sales division of a pharmaceutical company in London. I am someone with no problems in life and tension free. Well, other than my bullied past and nightmares, a lot of nightmares. But there were some people who always stood by my side and helped me escape bullying.

So, there was I brushing and bathing together. How did I do that? I didn't have time to think about it. I looked at the clock as it showed 8:00 a.m. and I had to be there by 8.40 a.m. It takes me an hour to travel from my apartment to my office. I wore my clothes and put on the deodorant and rushed down to the parking lot quickly.

I didn't worry about my breakfast because the office provides us breakfast from 8:40 a.m. to 9:00 a.m. There is lunch after 1:30 p.m. to 2:00 pm. I couldn't starve till lunch, as I had not eaten anything last night. So, I was driving down the busy city street with some bouts of fresh air and pollution.

Sometimes I look at the world around us and think what are they doing to a place that was so beautiful, but now a mess. I took a right and drove down towards the basement of this tall building called Maxcorp Towers. It is the seventh tallest building in the country. As I rolled down the slope I stopped at the kiosk and showed my card to the person sitting inside.

"Are you new in here?" I asked.

"No, why does everybody keep asking me that?" The person sitting inside said.

"Maybe because you have a new face ", I said.

He gave me a ticket and I pulled the switch on my hand rest and the glass slid up.

I found a spot and parked my sedan. I opened the door and stepped on the hard ground. The surrounding was extremely hot but bearable. I slammed the door of my car. I don't know why I did that. I walked towards the back of my car and opened the boot. It made a creaky noise as

BASEMENT PARKING

it opened. I remembered I have to get my car checked. I picked up my stuff and started walking towards the lift that leads to the ground level. As I was moving the ground beneath me started shaking.

CHAPTER II

I thought that it was just myself but then it happened again. It trembled for some more time and then it stopped. Everything became silent. It lasted for a few seconds and then suddenly a big piece of earth rose out of the surface and stood up like a tall cliff. It felt as if a monster had just been awoken from his sleep.

Everyone started to run.

BASEMENT
PARKING

The ground beneath me cracked and slabs of concrete started to fall from the ceiling. I just stood there, frozen. I started running towards the exit. It had got blocked. I heard some screams. I had no idea what was happening. I fell down face first having no clue what hit me. I lost my consciousness. It felt like I was extremely tired and I had just crashed on my bed. After a few seconds I could open my eyes. Everything was blurry and grey. With some difficulty I regained my vision and my consciousness.

This time it was for real. I felt some softness in my head. I sat up realizing that my head was lying in someone's hand. He withdrew it and asked me, " Are you all right?"

I remained silent for a while. Trying to let myself in the surroundings. The ceiling and the ground remained cracked. The air was filled with dust. I realized that a light was flashing. I tracked its origin and was astonished to know that the cars had survived. The light was flashing from one of its headlights. I heard a voice. I tried to figure out what was he saying. He said it again.

"Are you alright?"

The word "yes" slipped out of my mouth like butter. He asked me something else. After a few seconds I made out the words.

"Are you feeling any pain?"

"No".

I responded.

"What happened"? I asked.

"An earthquake." He said.

"Are you serious?"

"Of course I'm serious, how do you explain all this?"

It did make sense. This place was now not even a legitimate parking lot.

"All right, let's get you up".

That man said. He held my arm and helped me up.

“Thank you.” I said. Feeling a pain from somewhere. I ignored it.

“Please don’t mention it because I have to help a lot of people and I don’t think I can handle all the thanks.” He said.

“What’s to handle”? I ask.

“I don’t know”. He said.

“Come on, walk with me”.

“Ok”. I answered. I thought that he was giving me an order.

We started to walk. He walked slower compared to my speed. Maybe he was injured?

“My name is Tom, Tom Reynolds. And you?”

“Adam Robertson”.

“Ok”.

“How many people do you think survived”? I asked him.

“13 survived”.

“And how many are.......”

I hesitated to say the word dead. After a few seconds he interrupted me and said

“Dead”?

“Yes, dead.”

“I don’t know, we found a total of three dead bodies that we piled up in a corner so that we get more space to use up for treating injured people.”

“How many are injured”? “4”.

The word “dead” disturbed me somehow. It felt like we were doomed. I lost hope for five seconds but then thoughts of getting out of this place popped up in my mind, like the elevator or clearing out the boulders blocking the exit.

I asked him, “How long I’ve been out for?”

“Fifteen minutes, but why”?

“Follow me,” I said.

“Why”? He said

“I might just have a way to get out of here”, I said.

“Good, because we didn’t see to that.”

I started to jog towards the elevator that was some twenty meters away from where we were standing. As the breeze hit my face it also cleared my sweat a bit, making me feel better. He hesitated first but eventually started running behind me. When we reached the elevator, I saw the door bent and a few slabs fallen over it.

I looked at what was once the entrance of the elevator and saw concrete slabs piled on top of each other. They formed a small ramp making a small gap at the top.

I started climbing up the slabs with great difficulty as I slipped several times.

“What are you doing?” Tom said.

“Trying to climb up these slabs so we can find a way to get out of here”.

“Ok, but be careful”.

“Sure will”.

My head hit something hard as I climbed upwards.

“Owe”! I cried in pain as I was rubbing my head. I placed my hand above my head where my head got hit. I realized that the gap was covered by another slab. I climbed down and said

“The elevator route is trapped”.

“So”?

“So, one way of getting out of here is ruled out”? Tom questioned.

“Yes”, I said.

CHAPTER III

"How is the elevator route blocked"? Tom asked curiously. "As I was climbing up I hit my head on to a slab, only this time it was big and blocked."

"Oh, like that."

"Why did you say that?" I thought, if this was a joke to him and intended to ask this question but did not as he said, "I was wondering how could it be blocked?"

"Its logical". I responded.

"But it's still something that can be thought over".

Saying it in such a way that it felt as if nothing was happening around him. Suddenly somebody came jogging towards us. He had a strong and sturdy figure. He was a man for sure. He stopped at where we were standing and started to talk to Tom.

"Tom, I have some good news".

"What is it"?

"Three out of eight people are feeling better and after a few hours rest they should be fine".

"That's good news, but what about the other five?"

"They are still recovering".

"I'm sorry but who are you"? I interrupted

"Hi, my name is Jack and you"? He seemed friendly.

"Uh..." I hesitated again. Why do I do that?

"Uh, what"? Jack said, eager to know.

"Uh, Adam, I'm extremely sorry, it's just that since I've been here I'm just scared and I want to get out of here.

"I can understand, at least you aren't crying".

"That's good to hear".

"You might be glad, but other people are crying like anything".

The way he said that gave me a hope that maybe there might just be a way to get out of here. I thought of ramming the car through the slabs at the exit so that even if they do not break and make out a way for us, it could still weaken them and we can clear them out. I consulted this idea with Tom and Jack. They responded,

"Let's give it a shot".

Tom stood in between at the entrance and told everyone to clear out the way. His voice was so audible that it could be heard over a hundred feet, but unfortunately we had about forty-three feet of driving space. Our parking lot is fifty meters in length and thirty meters in breadth. According to the somewhat accurate calculations Tom had made, we might be able to weaken the rocks but there is a 20-30% probability that we might just break through. So, Jack and myself decided to go with that probability.

We searched for the fastest, unharmed and working car and we found a black BMW. There was an argument between Tom and Jack to decide who would ram the car. They both did not want to do it. This went on for some 10 minutes. Finally, I agreed to do it.

"Are you sure"?

"Yes, of course". I said, I didn't know why I felt so happy.

Tom got in the car and lined it up while Jack helped the injured people get on to the side. You must be thinking what was I doing meanwhile. I was chipping away through the slabs around the elevator. The elevator had been crushed because of the slabs and the debris helped me climb up easily as I discovered a route to go up. The tools that I was using to chip through the slabs were very small and blunt. There weren't any sharpening tools and the knife was becoming more blunt and it was slowing my speed. As I was chipping Jack pulled my pants and told me "we're ready".

CHAPTER IV

I walked towards the car. I decided to swag like a movie star readying for an action stunt, cause if I crash on to the debris, the slabs might drop on top of the car smashing my head. So if I was to go down, I might as well go down in style.

I sat in the black 320 and slammed the door. Tom bended down to the window and told me "Aim for the right side".

"Why not the middle"? I said, wondering why is he telling me to do that.

"Because the booth was there, so the debris might disturb you".

"Ok". I said, unsure.

I pushed the accelerator and the brake. The car roared like a lion. I shifted the gear up to five and let go of the brake. I sped down the road like a Cheetah trying to chase down a gazelle. I pushed down the accelerator all the way to the floor. I didn't thought of backing out and just before the car crashed on to the debris I opened the door and jumped out. I did not know where the strength came from. The adrenaline rushed down my spine. I landed on someone's hand. That guy was extremely strong to handle a 65 kg guy like me. I turned and saw the car slammed on to the debris of concrete and steel rods. Pieces of rocks went flying into the air. It was a completely different site than what you see in your day-to-day life. The crash did not make a lot of difference to the debris. It hardly weakened it.

I looked at the guy who caught me and I said, "Are you all right?"

"Yes, I am but the same could not be said about you".

"What are you saying"?

He stared at my right arm. I looked at it and I felt extreme pain. There was a big scratch on my arm. I started to scream in pain. Tom and Jack came running towards us.

"Are you fine"? He asked.

"My hand". I cried in agony.

Tom held my hand and lifted it up.

"Its just a cut".

"But it hurts so much".

"Ah, its nothing. Some spray and a tape and you will be fine in no time."

"Wait a minute, how do you know all this"? I asked.

"I was doing a part time job as a school doctor in the school nearby".

Tom told Jack to bring the first aid box from his car. Jack came rushing towards us and almost tripped when he stopped. It was like as if he was trying to run a 200m sprint with Usain Bolt.

Tom took out a spray from the black pouch that was handed to him by Jack. He sprayed that white bottle on my hand. It burned as if I was standing close to the sun. Then he rolled a tape on to my hand with some cotton stuck to it. He told me to take some rest for the next fifteen minutes. I leaned on to the pillar by my side and sat down. I spread my legs and tried to sleep. I don't know how I fell asleep in 15 seconds flat. When I woke up, I found Jack sitting beside me.

"How are you feeling"?

"Fine, just fine".

"He found a way".

"Who"?

"Tom".

CHAPTER V

"What are you talking about"?

"He was digging up the rocks at the stairs and he saw the door. He came down excitedly and told everyone that he just found a way."

"That's great news". I said happily, thinking that we may finally have a way to get out of this godforsaken place.

"But". He seemed upset.

I could see it in his face. Some thing disturbed him. The expression in his face looked like if someone had just died. The same thing had happened to me when my sister died. I had just the same face. I felt sad for him.

"What is it Jack?"

"Its just that.....".

He suddenly burst into tears. He cried as if a baby had lost his toy. I knew something bad had happened. So bad that it would affect me too. Well, actually in this case everything would affect me.

"What is it"? I asked.

"Come on, I'll show it to you". He cried.

He stood up and started walking towards the stairs. All the while he was sniffing and wiping his tears. I looked left and right and saw some people just awestruck. As if something indescribable had happened.

Some people were even crying, not thinking about the dust covered all over their bodies. That's when I realized that my body was covered in brown dust. Thankfully, I was wearing a black jacket, which I had to remove then. We reached the entry door of the stairs. It was green and completely filled with cracks.

"Look for yourself". He told me. Still sobbing like a baby.

I pushed the handle of the door. I swung it open. All of this I did in slow motion pace. As I stepped in, I froze.

I couldn't explain what I saw but I was still going to try. It was all red. Tom was lying there, lifeless. His body came beneath a huge concrete slab. The slab had crushed his body ripping his hands apart. I felt sad, shocked, scared, everything at once. Tears rolled down my eyes. I wiped them of. I couldn't say anything. I got out of there and started to climb up the slabs.

I slipped but I never stopped. Finally got to the door on the mezzanine level and opened it with great difficulty. As I opened it, I saw the exit was covered with blocks of concrete, from top to bottom.

I got upset. I wanted to scream, I wanted to punch someone in the face. I couldn't control myself. I climbed down and told Jack I would need some time. I got out of the stairs and started to run towards the main exit. The darkness somewhat blinded me. But I could still see where I was going. When I reached the exit I started to kick the blocks. I was on the left side of the exit. I kicked it so hard that my leg started to hurt. I kicked the slab at the bottom edge of it. I stopped to see some light. It shone from the extreme edge of the exit. I kicked it some more and the light got bigger. I lifted my leg once again and was about to kick when I saw a slab on the verge of falling down and covering the gap.

"Guys, come here", I yelled.

CHAPTER VI

Everybody came running towards me. Three or four of them simply just couldn't wake up cause they were too injured. The beats of their footsteps reminded me of the time when I had won the Interschool Cricket Championship. I was standing at the batsman's crease, legs bended, bat lifted at the back. My legs were shaking and sweat was running down my spine. I was frozen. I couldn't think about anything but how I am going to face that tall and thin fast pacer. He was extremely tall. We called him 'The Eiffel'. The Eiffel started to jog. That jog suddenly turned into a run. I started to feel cold as ice. He jumped and swung his arm. He threw the ball. It came towards me like a bullet. I stepped ahead, lifted my bat. I swung that piece of wood and clashed it with the cork and the ball went flying into the air, like an airbus taking off.

The ball went out of the ground and into the white colored complex next to it. Every one from my team came running towards me and lifted me up. They started cheering, “Adam! Adam! Adam!”

I came back to reality with Jack patting my back.

“Come back to reality man”. He said. Some of the others at the back were laughing at me.

“Ok”.

“Why did you call us in a hurry”.

“Check this out”.

I bent down and pointed at the gap.

CHAPTER VII

"How did you do it"? Jack asked.

"What did I do"? I was wondering what is he saying.

"The hole, you idiot". He said with a harsh tone. "I kicked the rocks".

"Oh". He said, finally coming back to a normal tone.

I bent down and I put my hand on the slab. It was very delicate, like the soft skin of a newborn. I lied down on my stomach and held the outer edge of the slab. The morning breeze of the city made my hands slightly colder, making me feel better. I pushed myself outside but got stuck halfway through. I shrugged and huddled to get out but all attempts failed. I pulled myself back. I sat up.

"I can't get out there, but a smaller and thinner guy can".

"But who can go out there over here".

I pushed Jack aside and looked for someone who is thinner. I couldn't get in there because I was healthy, not thin. I moved my head right and left but I couldn't find any one thin enough. I kept looking and then I saw someone thin enough who could get out but with a little effort. I rushed towards him.

"What's your name"? I asked.

He looked afraid. I asked him again.

"What's your name"?

"Andy". He said finally after hesitating.

"Ok Andy, are you injured?"

"No, but why?"

"Because you can get us out of here". I said with some hope.

CHAPTER VIII

"I don't understand". He said.

"Come with me", I said.

"Ok", he said, little confused.

He stood up with some difficulty even after my help. We went to the exit. I suddenly felt a little breathlessness. I stopped. Andy stopped too. He came to me.

"Are you all right"? He asked, putting his hand on my shoulder.

"I don't know, I can't breathe".

I put my hand on my neck and the other on my knee.

"Sit down". He said, and I did.

I couldn't breathe. Air didn't seem to reach my nostrils. I felt like I was in a pool and was drowning without any oxygen. Everything became blurred. The blurriness increased.

I saw Jack and some other people coming running towards me. After a few seconds I saw myself huddled up with some people. Jack and Andy to my shoulders.

The ground was shaking. Slabs were falling down. The ground was covering up quickly, making less space for us to stand. Then suddenly, the ceiling above us too cracked and in two seconds flat we were all pancakes.

I stood there seeing myself and others die a horrible death. I woke up screaming, “No”!!

4:38

Why do I have these nightmares every time I sleep? They have haunted my life since the day I was born. Every time I wake up I have a cuss word that spits out of my mouth. I saw Jack sitting beside me. It felt like déjà vu. It was just like when Tom died. Jack was again upset. Legs bent, one hand on the same knee and a weeping face.

"Why are you sad every time when I regain consciousness"? I said while getting up, annoyed by his look..

"The plan failed". He said.

"What do you mean failed"?

I heard a voice, brisk and harsh, although he was talking in a normal tone. It felt like he was screaming at me. I turned my head to the left side to see a tall, muscular figure. Combed hair, but turns to the right just above the forehead. He looked like a regular hero of a British action movie.

"Andy managed to crawl outside up to his hip but another earthquake occurred, causing the slabs and rocks to fall down but luckily we pulled him in just before a rock broke his back.

"I'm sorry but who are you"? I asked.

"Oh, Adam, Gabe. Gabe, Adam". Jack introduced.

"He helped me get you here", he said.

"Thanks Gabe", I said, trying to make myself look good.

"Don't mention it". He said, feeling proud of himself.

"So, what now?" questioned Jack.

CHAPTER IX

I stood up and scooted towards the main exit. I put my hands on the slab and hammered them. No luck. They weren't being affected. Suddenly, that breathlessness came again, luckily this time it was bearable. I called Jack and Gabe. Even Andy came along.

"Thought you might need my help".

"You're sure right about that".

"Are you feeling that"? I asked, maybe they were feeling breathless too. Not everybody's perfect.

"Yes". They said in a chorus.

"Okay, that means, we are losing oxygen". I said, thinking that this is going to get worse.

I started brainstorming, and then I tuned my head to Andy.

'Andy, tell everybody to get some sleep, if they can"?

"Jack, do you have a knife? He shook his head in negative.

"What about you Gabe"? He too shook his head.

"Andy", I yelled.

"Yeah", he replied.

"Ask them for a cutter or a knife".

I started knocking all over the slabs, trying to find a weak spot. I had seen it on the television. The guy was trying to get out of the place, so he started to find a weak spot and chipped his way through.

I saw Andy coming towards me with a steel knife. He handed it to me.

"Who gave this to you?" I asked curiously. Who would carry a knife in his car on his way to the office, was he planning a murder?

"Some guy named Prady, says he can help".

"Okay, call him. I'm sure we can use two more hands and legs".

He jogged and then disappeared.

"Adam can you please tell us what are you doing"? Gabe asked.

"I'm trying to chip a hole through so that we can get cell phone signal".

"Okay, can we be of any help?" Jack said.

"Not now, I don't need".

I kept flaking with the knife until a cold breeze of air hit my face. "I can see". I cried, finally having a hope to get out of here. They all came towards me and that Prady boy had also joined. They started pushing each other like kids to get a gasp of fresh air. But soon realized and queued up like grown ups.

"Hey Prady, go run to my car, it's the red sedan. Get in the car and you'll find a phone in the cup holder. Go get it fast".

He nodded and within two seconds he disappeared.

"What's your plan, don't be discreet. What are you trying to do"? Andy wondered.

"I'm trying to make a hole through the slab to get a signal, through which I can contact the authorities", I said.

I saw Prady coming out of the shadows.

He handed me the phone. I pressed the button on the side and then a bright light went into my eyes blurring my vision again. When it finally became normal, I was surprised to realize that the time was 12:30 pm. Remembering that I hadn't eaten anything for breakfast gave me a stomachache. I slid the display and the home screen appeared. It's interesting how technology improves day by day. I pressed the green icon with a telephone sign on it and a white screen appeared. I went to the keypad to dial 911. I put the phone to my ears to hear the ringer. After thirty seconds (which seemed like an hour) some body picked up and said

"911 what's your emergency?"

12
3
6
9

CHAPTER X

Hearing the voice on the other end made me so happy that I wanted to dance, scream and hug everyone. But then I controlled myself and decided to communicate with the person.

"911 what's your emergency"? She said again but this time her voice was broken.

I stood closer to the hole and then her voice became clearer.

"Yeah, hello, my name's Adam and we're stuck in a building's basement."

"How many people are there"?

I looked at Jack, remembering Tom.

I hesitated and said 14.

"Are you in the Maxcorp building"? She asked as if she knew something.

"Yeah, why?"

"Because an earthquake occurred in that area causing a few buildings to collapse.. We have some firefighters and police officers over there who will come and get you out.'"

"Thank you very much, but you've got to hurry because we're losing oxygen".

"Okay, sit tight we'll get you out." And then the phone beeped as it does every time the call ends. I put the phone in my pocket and saw that everybody was staring at me. I felt a little creepy but I didn't care. The excitement made me so happy that I didn't think about anything else.

"So"? Andy asked.

"They're coming". I said.

"Are you serious"? They said in a chorus.

"Yes". I said happily.

"Just find a way to pass the time and in 10 minutes, wake everyone up."

We all parted our ways. I went to my car, I saw Prady trying to take some rest and cuddling near a pillar. Gabe was standing beside the exit but Jack was nowhere to be seen. He must be with himself. After everything that had happened, a person trying to be alone with himself is not wrong at all.

I found a black sedan. A slab had demolished the boot of that car. But the front was still intact. I scooted towards the car. As I was nearing it, I felt that the air was getting thinner and thinner. But we could still breath. The car was parked at the right corner of the basement. I pulled the door open and threw myself in the drivers seat. I was exhausted and famished and thirsty. I decided to wait for some time. But it was unbearable. Luckily I saw a bottle of water filled in it. I stretched my hand and as I was about to pick it the door swung open. It was like as if my treasure was taken away from me.

I saw a hand picking up that bottle of water and tossing it in my hand. I sat upright and opened the bottle cap in a jiffy. Just as I opened it, Gabe jumped in the car causing a mild *carquake* and spilling ¼th of the water on me.

"Oops". He chuckled.

I drank the water fast and with a big relief, I said,

"Phew, now that's a bottle of water".

"That's not just a bottle of water, that's *my* bottle of water. Luckily, I have two more".

He picked up a larger bottle of water and drank all of it and laughed after seeing me frozen.

"I'm sorry, I'm a heavy drinker. I can't do anything about it. I'm like a camel". He laughed. I punched him in the stomach.

"That was not funny". I said in a harsh tone.

He reached for the second bottle. That guy's unbelievable.

"HEY, leave it for the others". I was cross.

"Calm down man". He said.

He was right. I should.

"So, what are you going to do after this"?

"I don't know. I just want to doze off for 20 hours without any nightmares and forget all of this". I said with meaning every word I said.

CHAPTER XI

"Yeah, that's something that I would like to do", I said.

"I wish that this would have never happened. But something tells me that this was planned for me, to pay the price for my crimes that I committed in the past, but I can't relate anything to this".

"Did you do anything like it"? Gabe asked.

"I don't know". Trying my best to get back my memories from my childhood. I had a great childhood. I received good education and then went to Cambridge for further studies.

As I tried to think, I remembered something that had happened during the first semester of my college.

It was a late evening, and the breeze had a chill in it. Everything was peaceful and quiet except for the chirping of birds, and water sprouting from a nearby fountain. The quietness was then disturbed by a group of bullies who had picked on a boy. These guys were famous for their bullying. They were called the MBG (Major Bullying Group). Some guy in the first semester of the college had started this group. A tall guy named Bill Stacey, started beating a guy and broke his leg. Some people got inspired and were recruited by him and they formed the MBG. Eventually they were rusticated but some other people continued it.

They went down the stairs that led to the sports ground near the forest. I decided to follow them. If they were up to something, I would catch them red handed. The MBG had been quiet for a long time. I could finally have some evidence.

I skipped down the stairs. Everything was dark and eerie. I saw five people carrying the tiny guy on their shoulders. After a few seconds I saw them drop him onto the ground. The leader put his hands on his pockets and pulled something out, something unexplainable.

He pulled out a gun. It was a small Walther. Where in the world did he get a gun? I saw him point out the gun to the guy's head. Was the piece real? He gripped it and pulled the trigger. The sound of the bullet leaving the chamber echoed all around the campus. The bullet pierced through his head. The shooter was pushed back. They all ran away immediately. I stood there, frozen; I turned around and then started walking.

A half an hour later, the police came followed by media. Everybody was sent home. No one knew what happened. The next week everyone in the school was called for questioning. The gang was caught. But I never spoke up. This is the only regret in my life that I have ever had and I'm trying to forget that. It was after then I started to get nightmares every night.

All this time, while I was telling my story to Gabe, he did not utter a word nor did he interrupt. He just sat there and listened. After a few seconds of silence he said. "Wow, I would have never imagined what you might have been through and that your past causes you trouble and makes you sad. The least you can do is stay calm and forget, but that would be cowardice. In your case I don't have anything to say".

"It's ok, I did not expect you to understand."

I heard somebody panting and running. I looked outside to see Prady running towards us. He caught his breath and said,"They're here".

CHAPTER XII

"Look, now's not the time for jokes, all right". Gabe said. He seemed very angry.

"Ok, look for yourself". Prady said.

I got out of the car and ran towards the entrance. The excitement made my speed increase.

Once I got there I peeked through the hole and saw a guy yelling in a loudspeaker. I made out the words "Please back up, we are going to break the exit. You have one minute." To the left I saw a big crane holding a wrecking ball. I turned my back.

"EVERYBODY WAKE UP", I yelled.

Everybody got a shock. Even Andy.

"Everybody stand at the back, we're going to get out of here."

Every one was tired. After around 15 seconds they got up.

They all slowly moved towards the back and started to stare at me with a demi-god kind of a look.

I went back to stand along with them and heard Andy whispering into my ears.

"What are you going to do after you get out".

"I don't know, sleep I guess".

"That's the best you can think of".

Before I said anything I heard a loud noise that stunned me. The ground started shaking beneath me.

Everybody started running. I looked ahead. The light weakened my eyes. After my eyes got adjusted, I started running too. The slabs had started to fall again. Some fire fighters were assisting people to get out. Just before I went out of the half blocked exit, I heard a cry. I thought I was hallucinating but I looked at the back. There, I saw Prady's leg stuck by a rock. I looked ahead to see two firefighters yelling at me to get out. Ignoring them, I ran towards Prady. A person who I don't even know, why would I try to help him? But after all, he is still a human who has a life.

I went near Prady and tried to move the rock. The shaking ground helped me move the rock away. I lifted him up with great difficulty. I started to run. It seemed like forever but as I got closer to the exit my speed decreased. As I got nearer to the exit I felt the smell of the city. I finally reached the exit but then again everything blacked out. No pain. I couldn't feel anything. I just finally got a chance to breathe some clean air.

CHAPTER XIII

I woke up to an extremely white place. Almost everything was white. People in white clothes were walking everywhere holding a pad in their hands. I sat up to realize that I was in a white bed.

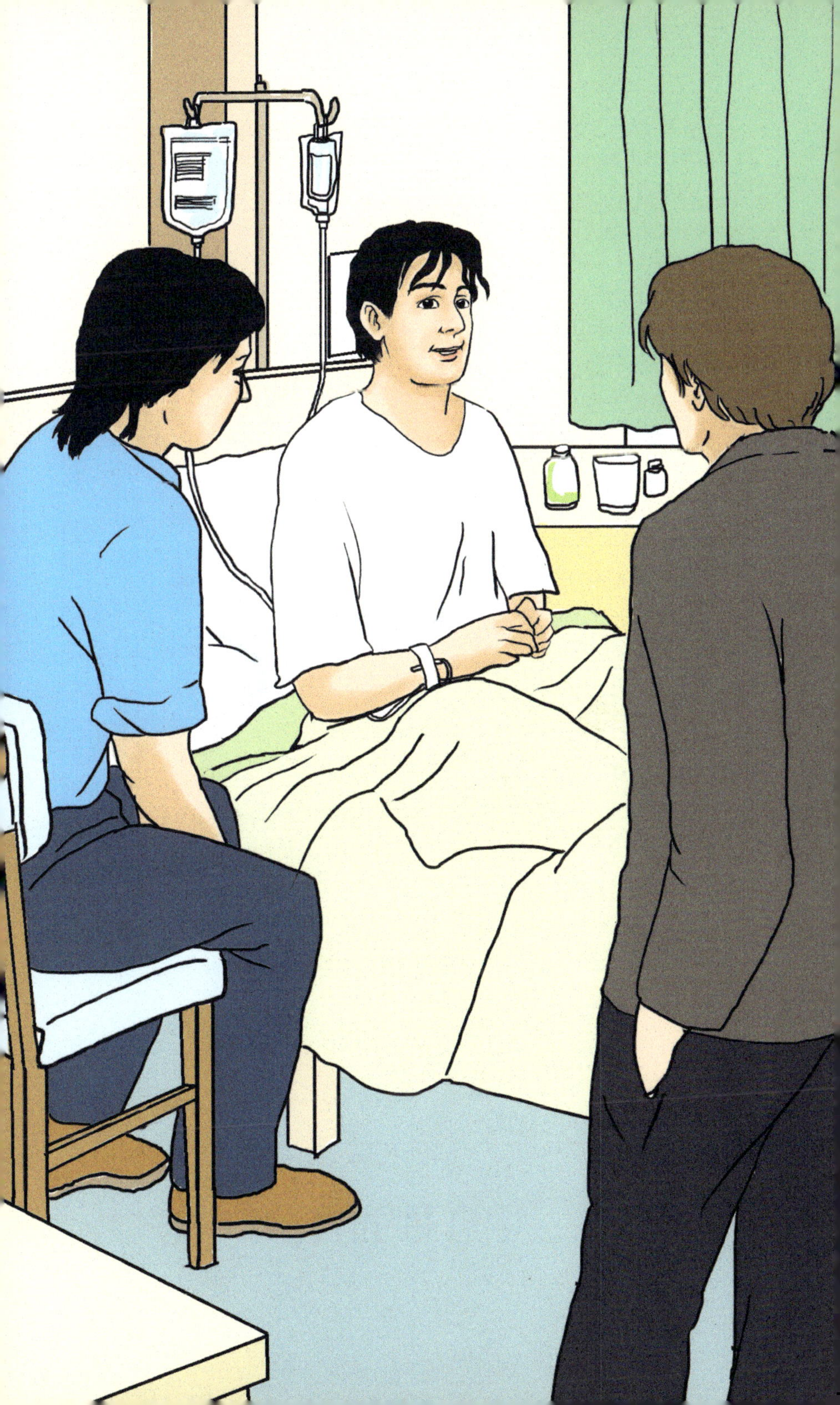

I was in a hospital. I felt surprised that this was one sleep without any nightmares. None. That felt really good.

I heard a sound of a woman. I turned my head to the left and looked up. That voice was emanating from the television nearby. I heard the lady saying,

"A young man named Adam Robertson played a major role in rescuing 14 people from the basement of an office building".

"So, we're out". I heard Jack's voice.

I turned my head to the right to see him sitting on a stool. This was the first time I saw him happy after I became conscious.

"Yes, we are". I said happily.

"Where are all the others"? I asked him, worried.

"Well, they are being treated by doctors. Prady broke his leg. The doctor said there's nothing much to worry about".

"Great, just great". I said.

"So, how does it feel like to be a hero".

"What do you mean"?

"I mean, everybody is talking about you, calling you the local hero", he said

Hearing that made me feel so happy.

"Feels awesome". I said.

"That's what I wanted to hear". Jack said.

"That's what I wanted to be".

I lied down and closed my eyes content fully..... no more afflictions of the past.

THE END

CPSIA information can be obtained
at www.ICGtesting.com
Printed in the USA
LVOW01s1108221016
509749LV00035B/222/P